Many thanks to-my family for all their support. A huge thank you to Tony De La Rosa, Angela Richardson, Tracy Piland, Detective Tori-Lynn Heaton and Lillan Rodriguez-Talley.

Also to all of you, my friends (aka extended family) whom have been with me from the beginning, cheering me on and supporting my creative endeavors. I truly cannot thank you all enough.

Peace and Blessings
Carlos (Los) Espada

Authors Note

The story you're about to read is one that I wrote with every free waking moment I could spare. I would write on the train ride to and from work, during lunch breaks and of course, staying up all night to work (or in this case write) is not uncommon for me.

The idea for this story came from a deep place. At the time the news was reporting on women who suffer from postpartum depression and psychosis. I would hear co-workers and strangers write it off, mainly due to lack of understanding.

Depression overall is dismissed not only by strangers but sadly, by family and friends as well.

Which cuts the deepest.

My greatest hope is that this story will help others to not only take the time to understand the many levels of depression, but also to stop using the phrase "Get over it."

Depression can affect anyone, your race, sex or religious beliefs do not exclude you.

I myself suffer from depression. It is not something we can turn on and off at will.

It can be completely crippling. Being utterly alone to battle such demons is never a good feeling.

I have lost friends to depression and I sometimes wonder, if someone (including myself) would have spoken with them, and more importantly listened to them, would they still be here today?

I can only hope to give you some idea as to what someone can go through and the effects it can have on both the individual and those around them.

Love and unity
Carlos (Los) Espada

Chapter 1

The brightly-lit cafe is decorated with photos of famous people who have come into the shop over the years. The bus boys are taking down New Year's decorations while people sit around in linen-covered wood booths eating, drinking and speaking between bites and sips. Among them is a tall man with black hair and a fair complexion. He slumps over his laptop while transferring notes from the screen into a black and white composition notebook. Adjacent to his other paperwork sits a cold cup of half-finished coffee. The coffee often competes for attention as the man scribbles notations in hurried shorthand.

Eric Bisley, enjoys coming to the Black Star coffee shop in order to get some thinking done and often conducts business meetings by phone while he waits for his meal. He's been a frequent patron of this coffee shop for nearly six months; three times a week on Mondays, Wednesdays, and Fridays. Eric has grown accustomed to the usual greetings from the waitresses when he comes in. The friendly Hello! What can I get you? just about completes the exchange of routine pleasantries between waitress and customer. That was until a new waitress arrived two weeks before Christmas.

Janeane's soft wavy blonde tendrils complement the sense of innocence in her eyes, which are framed by stylized metal glasses pushed high up on the bridge of her nose. She is a curvaceous thirty something with an infectious smile and a wry sense of humor. Since Janene began working at the Black Star, Eric has stepped up his coffee shop visits. On the many occasions when their eyes have met, smiles tentatively widen and eyes lock in momentary pairings of possibility. Then, just as suddenly, they both look quickly away. On this particular afternoon, while making her rounds, Janene decides to engage Eric in conversation. Stopping at his booth, she takes a breath and says.

"Good morning and Happy New Year."

Eric lifts his head almost too shy to make eye contact with the attractive waitress. In contrast to his usual confidence, he seems to lose his composure whenever Janeane nears his booth. To help calm his nervousness, he fidgets with the lid of a Tic Tac box, rapidly opening and closing the lid. In an attempt at humor, Eric shouts:

"Merry New Year!"

Delighted that he isn't as rigid as his workaholic habits would suggest, Janeane quickly fires back.

"Oh Wait!... I know that movie......Don't tell me....."

After a few seconds of searching her brain for the answer, Janeane gives up.

"Ok. Just tell me."

Eric's smile widens and he replies, "Drum roll, please. That's correct ladies and gentlemen, it's...Trading Places."

Janeane giggles.

"Ohhhh!! See, I knew that. So, how come you're always here? In the movie business? "

Finding a sense of comfort in Janene's eyes, Eric shyly, responds.

" Usually it's more practical to work from home, but once in a while I need to get outside of those four walls. I come here because, you know, it's quiet and I can get a lot done."

Janeane leans in a bit to refill Eric's cold cup of half-finished coffee.

"Nothing like the clatter of plates and glassware to set the tone for efficient work, huh? He smiles.

"Seriously, I'll let you get back to work. By the way, my name is Janeane. Call if you need anything else. Eric joking replies:

"How can I? I don't have your number."

Suddenly uncomfortable at the impulsive return of his confidence, Eric follows up the remark with a sincere expression and barely audible monosyllabic phrases.

"Yeah. Bad joke. Sorry."

Janeane reassures him with a smile and walks away toward the counter where two other waitresses have been pretending not to watch the interaction from a distance. Lillian, a curvy Latina with long black hair can barely wait for Janeane to reach the counter. Lillian is somewhat of a drama queen and knows the scandalous details of all her customers because she lingers[1] deliberately at tables long enough to catch snippets of private conversations. She hasn't been able to get anything on Eric since he is always alone and usually too busy to talk.

"Damn gurl, you got the only cheese smile!"

Janene does not take the bait but her playfully seething glare says that the boisterous waitress should lower her voice.

The other waitress, Sabrina, is a petite woman of Asian and Afro-American heritage. As an aspiring actress, she often needs someone to take over her shifts and Janeane willingly covers whenever asked. As a result, she and Janeane have become close. Sabrina chimes in:

"She always gets different when he's around!"

Neither waitress bothers to conceal their enjoyment. They elbow each other and giggle loudly. Janeane's cheeks are almost crimson now.

"Shhhh, you two. God!! He's gonna hear you."

Janeane points at Lillian.

"Especially you big mouth." They all start to laugh.

Janene begins to straighten menus on the countertop while whispering in a conspiratorial manner.

"He is cute but... I'm not ready to meet anyone."

Sabrina shoots/fires a puzzled look at Janeane.

"Why? What's the hold up? Your ex is long gone."

Lillian joins in.

"He wasn't right for you anyway. This guy here at Table 5...he has got it together. Well, it looks like he does anyway."

Janeane looks down at the speckled black and silver linoleum.

"My daughter and I made a pact. That last guy was a nightmare and she despised him. I can't just bring a nice guy in behind that drama. Especially if I'm not ready."

Sabrina gently places a hand on Janeane's shoulder:

"It's a new day, luvvy. You can't live in the past. Think about it. It can't hurt to get to know the guy. He may surprise you." Janene Simmons has recently moved back to the same Chelsea neighborhood that hosted seven years of tumultuous marriage and the birth of a beautiful baby girl. Back then, there was a two-story duplex boasting a magnificent view of lower Manhattan. Back then, familiar sounds of quiet early morning enveloped Janene as she sipped warm cups of cappuccino and contemplated her charmed yet tumultuous life. This time around the digs weren't as spacious, but the tiny flat that she shared with her now teenage daughter had a sense of serenity that could never have existed in the other apartment. The view now might not be as grand but it suited her part-time writing efforts. The rest of the time she spent working at the Black Star café. It was within walking distance of her apartment, which gave Janene plenty of opportunity to walk and be inspired by the city she loved.

Chapter 2

The next mid-morning Eric is back at the coffee shop in his usual booth. The booth is positioned on the side of the shop that has windows facing the pier. He enjoys the notion of boats docking after a long voyage. Mostly though, there is the same ancient gray battleship permanently sitting in the same place. Eric likes to imagine that it is waiting to be boarded before setting off for some far away place. He considers the type of passengers on such a voyage as he begins to unpack his briefcase. From across the coffee shop, Janeane spots him and carefully moves toward his station to avoid spilling the steaming cup of coffee she has prepared for him. Knowing Eric's daily routine by now, Janene has taken the liberty of anticipating his order. She hopes he will not be offended at the gesture.

Maybe I should just let him order like usual. No, he still has to place his order for whole wheat toast and two eggs. He shouldn't mind. Well, what if he does? I am being considerate, not pushy.

Eric notices the confused look on her face and the cup of coffee with vapors of steam rising from it. He pushes the notepad and briefcase over just as she arrives at the table.

"Good morning. Welcome back."

With a smile, he greets her in return. "Good morning!"

To Janeane's critical eye, Eric appears flustered.

"You okay?"

Responding to the warmth in her voice, Eric stops and looks directly into her concerned eyes.

"Yeah, just have to problem-solve with a company overseas that I'm writing for. People change their minds like they change their underwear."

She has set the cup of coffee on the table and reaches for her order pad. Trying not to sound too interested, she says,

"Oh.... so that's what you do!"

"Yea. I set words to music so that a company's product will be more memorable than the other guy."

Janene pauses for the briefest part of a moment as she realizes that her heart is beginning to increase its pace. Eric starts to fumble with the lid of a Tic Tac box, which seems always near at hand. click...click – click...click.

"So, may I ask what you write about?"

Eric likes the sound of her voice. It is a combination of sensual smoothness and strength accompanied by an unmistakable tenderness. "If you promise not to laugh"

Janeane looks directly into Eric's sea-green eyes and thinks to herself that she could easily tell him almost anything.

After tracing an x over her heart, she affirms, "I promise." Eric leans in toward Janene, takes a deep breath and says, "I write jingles for x-rated products."

"X-rated product jingles"? Like, for sex toys?"

Unable to contain himself, Eric chuckles.

No. Companies hire me to write songs for their upcoming products. Usually, I work on food products that are sold in international markets where jingles still contribute to sales. Some great, some not so much."

Intrigued Janeane replies:

"Anything I would know?"

Eric smiles "Sadly, I am sure you wouldn't."

Janene's interest has been piqued.

"Ok. Let me hear one and I'll tell you if I know it."

Eric takes another deep breath.

"Are you really going to shame me into this?"

Janeane displays an impish smile.

"Yup!"

Eric clears his throat before diving into a barely audible verse from one of his more famous coffee jingles.

Wake up,

Get up

Time to move your feet!

Eric falters, begins again and starts to laugh heartily. In a mock display of pleading, he joins his two hands together in front of his chest.

"I beg you. Don't make me sing."

Janeane's smile broadens as she considers his willingness to make a fool of himself in a public place in order to please here. Sabrina was right. He had surprised her and that hadn't happened with a man in a very long time. With this light-hearted exchange over with, it was time for Janene to get back to work. Although there had been a lull after breakfast, it was now approaching noon and the lunch crowd would soon keep her busier than she liked to be. Not knowing exactly what else to say, she flips to a blank page in her order pad, motions her head in the direction of the kitchen, and waits for Eric's order.

"Oh, right. Whole wheat toast and two eggs, sunny side up.

Hoping that there might be a possibility of a yes, he adds, "And if I could get a phone number to go that would absolutely make my day."

Not sure what to expect, Eric looks down toward the table and then summons the courage to fix Janene with a more serious gaze. "I mean, if it's not too forward to ask. I would really like to get to know you. Maybe a movie or a bite to eat? I am sure that you get the same request a million times, but, I promise not to put the moves on you... till our second date. That is, if you say yes? "

Janeane finishes scribbling the food order in her notepad and then turns to another blank page in the notebook.

"I will get this order in. It should only take a couple of minutes. In the meantime, maybe you want to settle up at the register now."

She places the check face down on the table and walks away.

Not sure what had just happened, Eric reaches for the check and finds that there are two slips. The first one was scribbled with coffee/ww toast/ss eggs, and the second slip had ten large numbers neatly written on it along with a smiley emoticon in the corner next a big J.

Chapter 3

It is a bright Saturday afternoon at the beginning of January. The temperature hoovers around fifty-three degrees as Eric and Janeane sit close together on a park bench after their movie date. Along with the usual weekend cacophony of children shouting, carriages rolling over pavement, and the incessant honking of New York taxi horns, there is the click...click...click...click of a Tic Tac lid held absentmindedly in Eric's ungloved hand.

Janene has endured the habit for as long as she could and now says mockingly, "OK, I have to ask. What's with the Tic Tac lid?"

Eric stops immediately and shoves the container into the pocket of his winter jacket. Blushing, he says, Blushing

" I guess I'm nervous."

Janeane smiles. "Me too."

They realign themselves so that their knees feel fused together. Janene links her arm through Eric's coat sleeve and settles in against the warmth of his compact build. In turn, Eric welcomes the intimacy of their nearness. He thinks about the old grey battleship sitting at the dock in the same place and is sure that he could sit where he is forever if Janene were with him. The effect of this thought causes a full and comforting feeling to stir in the hidden places of Eric's heart. He smiles deeply before speaking. So, tell me about yourself. I know you are a waitress. What else is there to know about Janeane?"

Not yet ready to disclose all there was to know about herself, she begins with a theatrical excitement in her voice.

"We'll, I love to write and could, were it not for waitressing, write for days on end. I love Romance novels and Do-It Yourself projects."

She pauses for a second and bites her lip tentatively. Settling into a more solemn mood, she withdraws her arm from Eric's and places her hands in her lap. "Eric, I need to tell you something and I am not sure how to say it, so I just will. I have a 14-year old daughter. Her name is Anna.

Janene waits a moment for the new information to sink in before continuing. "I know lots of men don't want to be with a single mother. I need to know if that's a deal breaker."

Not wanting to lose the nearness of her touch, Eric reinserts her arm through his, and gently rubs her gloved hand before responding in a casual tone.

"So, what do you write about?"

As her smile widens and her shoulders relax, she moves closer to Eric's strong frame.

"Poetry mostly... though I have been working on this comedy based on my job as a waitress. Maybe you could read it? If you like?"

Eric is relieved to hear the concern drop from Janeane's voice.

"That would be great. If you like? It so happens that I know some people who may be able to help publish it as well. No promises, but it can't hurt to try."

Janeane turns toward Eric and holds him in a gaze mixed with appreciation and disbelief.

"Really? I mean, only if you want to and if you even think it has potential."

Eric could not have been happier at the prospect of being around this woman and earning her trust.

"I'm sure I will."

Janeane suddenly feels a tinge of uncertainty. She abruptly repositions herself and withdraws her arm from Eric again. As she faces him, he could see the light in her chestnut eyes dim. She sat up causing her leg to move

away from his. The distance, although slight, feels to Eric like a chasm. She fixes him with the most serious expression he has yet to see. "There's just one major rule."
Eric braces himself.
"Just one rule? Lay it on me."
Janeane continues.
"I would like to wait before I introduce you to my daughter. Please say you understand."
It is now Eric's turn at theatrics. He jolts up from the bench and feigns a startled posture.
"Noooo, I can't. Anything but that!
Janeane, surprised at Eric's unexpected movement, remains immobile and confused. Several uncomfortable moments pass before the confusion is broken as Eric launches into a robust chuckle.
"Kidding. I totally get it. I have to get pass Mama Bear's test. Eric reaches down to pull Janene up from the park bench.
"I don't plan on going anywhere, Miss Poetry-writing Waitress. That is if you want me around. Janeane throws her arms around Eric's neck and buries her face in his winter jacket.
"God, where did you come from?"
Their mutual hug lasts long enough for Janene to gain control over the flow of emotions that threaten to overtake her. Eric, sensing her need to hold on, continues to enjoy the extent of the embrace. He moves one blond tendril from her forehead and kisses her once, twice and again. Then, he takes Janene's hand in his and heads toward the curb to hail a cab. It has been a meaningful afternoon. One he would not soon forget.

Chapter 4

T he next morning Janeane knocks on Anna's bedroom door.
"Come on sleepy head time to wake up. We have lots to do today.
Gotta start our spring cleaning."
The door opens and Janeane's daughter walks out of the bedroom rubbing
her eyes. "Ma," she says groggily, it's Saturday. Why are you even awake?"
Janeane stops setting the table for breakfast, walks over and kisses her
daughter on the forehead.

"Because my love, I wanna do something fun today. A book store followed
by a pizza, then home to get this place cleaned up."
Anna pulls out the chair and flops into it. Janeane pours Anna some corn
flakes and takes the seat across from her.

"Sounds like fun Ma."
In the next moment, something occurs to Anna.

"Ohhhhhh Ma! Can we see Friends with Benefits?
Janeane works to keep from spitting out her coffee and manages to swallow
it before responding.

"Get the freak outta here! You are too young for that type of movie, silly.
Finish eating... I'm gonna jump in the shower."
Janeane heads for the bathroom while Anna returns to her sullen morning
temperament. The cell phone on the kitchen table chirps. Anna picks up
her mother's phone and sees a text message from Eric Bisley. Who is Eric?
Anna says half to herself while cautiously looking over her shoulder to see

if her mother has heard the ringtone or the question. She reads: Hi my beautiful girl, thinking of you! MUAH.

Anna lays the cell phone down when she hears her mother's bare feet heading back toward the kitchen.

"Forgot my cell phone," says Janeane.

"Expecting a call in the shower, Ma?"

"No, well. Why haven't you finished eating yet.

Anna puts the spoon down and folds her arms across her chest. Fixing her mother with a scornful glare, she fights to hold back the torrent of emotions that quickly build up behind her eyes.

Noticing her daughter's silent defiance, Janeane asks, "What's wrong my luv?"

Anna points at her mother's cell phone with an accusatory finger. Janeane reads Eric's text message and takes a deep breath. She had hoped to have more time to figure out a way to approach the topic of Eric with Anna. Now, she was out of time. As Janene grasps at ways to diffuse her daughter's apparent anger and confusion, Anna unfolds her arms and pushes up from the table abruptly. The movement sends milk cascading over the edge of the bowl and onto Janene's phone. Janeane senses the beginning of (yet another) argument and secures the bath towel around her shapely frame before sitting down to take the full dose that Anna is about to deliver. She considers whether to pick up the phone and dry it off before the milk damages it. The thought is interrupted by Anna's severe tone.

"I thought we would talk about it? You know…before you would just date someone! Why can't you just be honest with me? I don't keep things from you. And, what is up with muah? Have you slept with him already?"

Janeane felt as if the roles had been reversed and she were a child being brought to task for an unforgivable infraction. She knew Anna had been through it with the last guy and would not be thrilled with any next one, but to find out this way only made explaining things more difficult. Janeane stood up attempting to place her hands on Anna's shoulders. Sensing her mother's intended gesture, Anna pulled back out of Janeane's reach and moved away toward the refrigerator. Anna's reaction hurt Janeane in a way that only a child's accurate fault finding can injure a parent. The only thing to do now was to be honest.

"Anna, I know we went through a lot with the last boyfriend. I know it hurt you as much as it hurt me. But you need to believe me when I tell you that I haven't been with anyone since because I saw how hard you took it. You mean everything to me and I don't want to see you hurt like that again."

Anna reluctantly pulls out a kitchen chair and sits on the opposite side of the table from her mother.

"So, where did you meet this one?"

Grateful that her daughter had resigned her hostile stance in favor of sarcasm, Janeane replies in a soft tone.

"At the coffee shop. He's a musician of sorts and a really nice and thoughtful man. He knows that I have a daughter who means the world to me and he is okay with taking it slow. Honest honey, I didn't want you to find out this way. I wanted to talk to you first."

Anna could feel the tears begin to build behind her eyes and fought to hold on to the position her mother's omission of facts had granted her. She felt justified in her anger and was not yet ready to let her mother off so easily.

"What were we going to talk about? Would it have made a difference, Ma? You've already made up your mind."

Seeing Anna's eyes well up, Janeane tries to explain further.

" What do you want me to do? I'm trying here for both of us."

Anna feels exhausted as the disappointment and sadness compete for her emotional attention. No longer able to hold out, she shouts a tearful reproach at her mother.

"YOU COULD GO BACK TO DADDY! Why can't you make it work?"

Equally drained, Janeane sits down next to Anna and is encouraged when the teen does not venture to move away. Pushing the soft blond tendrils away from her own face, Janeane considers her daughter's distraught expression framed by a mass of thick auburn hair. With a motherly tenderness, Janeane rearranges a section of hair, placing it behind Anna's ear. Hesitantly, she begins the same monologue she has given since Anna's father left them both.

"We both know that's not gonna happen, my love. You know your father has been seeing someone else. He doesn't have time for us. He never did." Anna shoots up from the table, unsettling the napkin holder, and storms out the room. Resolved not to increase her daughter's pain, Janeane remains in the kitchen where she stares out of the small window above the sink before resting her face in her hands. Crying for her daughter's unhappiness as well as the happiness she might find with Eric, Janeane moves to set right the overturned napkin holder. She pulls one out, blows her nose, and discards it before picking up the cell phone. Droplets of milk have not damaged it and a quick wipe across her towel dry the device off. After staring at the phone, Janeane sits up straight in the chair and dials Eric's number.

"Hi, I'm ok. Listen, I can't do this right now. I am sorry. This is good bye." Janeane hangs up the phone, lays her head on the table and begins to cry again. Hearing her mother's continual sobbing, Anna peeks into the kitchen but does not enter. Sure that there was nothing that she could say or do that would make her mother feel better, Anna turns around and walks back to her bedroom. She closes the door quietly on her mother's unhappiness.

Chapter 5

It is a rainy Friday afternoon in February at the Black Star. Things are generally quiet on the weekends as the work crowd abandons the coffee shop in favor of more fitting end of week venues. Today is no exception. The sound of raindrops cascading across awnings and pattering against concrete continue in metered consistency as the waitresses sit at a back booth refilling salt and pepper shakers. Janeane enjoys the quiet and the uncomplicated task of filling what is empty. In spite of herself; however, every time she hears the door open, Janeane turns in the hopes of seeing Table 5's regular customer. Her preoccupation is broken by Lillian.

"Sooooo,gurl! What's going on with you and your man?"

Janeane avoids eye contact.

"Nothing, I had to break it off."

Sabrina is visibly shocked by Janeane's off-handed delivery of the statement as if she were placing an order for a BLT.

"What?! Why?"

Lillian chimes in "What are you crazy? That boy is a catch!"

Janeane continues to watch the door while filling the shakers. She takes a napkin and tries to stop the tears from falling. "I know,but my daughter is freaking out about it and it's best to let him go. He doesn't need that drama. She's still hung up on the idea of me and her father getting back together."

Sabrina reaches over and holds Janeane's hand.

"Listen mama, you and that man have been clocking each other for months.

I see how you light up when he walks in. You have been standing here in a daze."

Lillian interrupts "Gurl you are staring at that door every two seconds. He's not gonna walk through it. He hasn't been here."

Janeane looks over at Lillian. With the sound of disappointment. "He hasn't?"

Sabrina drives the point home.

"Nope! You better go get him, before someone else does. True love doesn't show its face but once in a life time."

Lillian jokingly adds in.

"Gurl, you can't put a good man on lay-away. Good men are so hard to find."

Janeane nervously replies, "I can't my daughter..."

Sabrina interrupts.

"...will grow to understand. Don't let that stop you, mama. You deserve to be happy. If he is willing to be with you and was willing to wait to meet your daughter, I'd say he's a keeper."

Janeane bites her bottom lip, deep in thought.

"Can you guys watch my tables? I have a phone call to make."

Both waitresses smile. Lillian playfully shoves Janeane.

"Go, we got you. Get your man!"

Janeane walks to a quiet corner and dials Eric's number. She gets his voice mail.

"Please call me, I wanna talk to you. Can you stop by my job? I miss you!"

She walks back to where the waitresses are standing.

"So?" Lillian excitedly asks.

"Did you talk to him?"

Janeane sounds disappointed.

"No. He must be working. This sucks, what if he doesn't come back to me? What if he found someone else?"

Sabrina hugs her.

"He will, if it's meant to be. You two will find one another."

Janeane's phone goes off. She scrambles for her phone to read the text message. Sabrina looks at Janeane like, Well? Janeane nods her head yes! The girls give her the thumbs up.

"It's a text from Eric! He said ok. He'll meet me. Shit!!! I need make-up. I look like a mess."

Lillian in her booming voice says, "You look fine gurl!"

Sabrina slaps Janeane on the back.

"Thanks, Daily News. Now the whole place knows it too."

Janeane grabs her bag and turns to the waitresses

"Please watch my tables. I have to change and meet him. Wish me luck. I am so nervous."

Both girls reply in unison. "GO!!!! He'll be happy to see you."

Janeane runs out the door. Lillian turns to Sabrina.

"If that doesn't work out. I'm soooo hooking him up with my sister." Sabrina has a look of disgust on her face when she asks. "Who? Nancy? Ewwwww!

Chapter 6

Inside Janeane's apartment, Eric is sitting on the couch while Janeane is in the kitchen. Eric looks over at Janeane as she is cooking. He smiles at the sight of her profile.

"So, how has the writing been going?"

Janeane replies without breaking her stride.

"I been trying, but with my daughter and work it's kind of hard to get any down. Listen, I have my daughter coming home soon. I told her she would be meeting you. I gotta warn you she has an attitude most of the time. Even with some of her guy friends."

With a jokingly cocky tone in his voice.

"No worries, I got a way with kids. Plus, I am a good looking."

Janeane laughs "You are too much, silly boy."

Janeane hears keys at the front door. She looks nervously at Eric and gives him a final warning.

"Here she comes! Please excuse her if she isn't talkative."

Eric just smiles as the door opens and Anna walks in. Janeane introduces Anna to Eric.

"Anna, this is Eric. Eric, this is my daughter, Anna."

Eric stands up and shakes Anna's hand.

"It is a real pleasure to meet you. How was your day?"

Anna looks down avoiding eye contact and in a soft voice replies

"Hi, it was ok. I guess."

As Janeane watches the interaction between the two, she starts to see smoke coming from the kitchen.

"Oh damn! The pork chops!"

Janeane runs into the kitchen. Anna takes a seat across from Eric still avoiding eye contact. Eric tries to ease the tension.

"So.... your mother tells me you play guitar?"

Anna replies in a soft voice. "A little."

Eric inches forward on the couch.

"My first instrument was bass guitar. Which stunk, because I couldn't play anything for friends and family. There aren't too many recognizable bass lines. You dance as well?"

Anna smiles and begins to open up.

"Yeah! We have a show coming up at my school before summer vacation. I got to pick the music!"

Janeane sneaks a look at the two conversing and smiles. Neither one of them notices Janeane as they continue to talk.

"NICE! You gotta be good to be running stuff at school, huh?"

Anna laughs a little.

"No.... It was just my turn to pick the song."

Eric continues. "So, have you tried playing a song? Maybe write one on guitar? Do any of your friends play instruments?"

"Nah, Well...My friend plays the drums but really not well," Anna says in her soft voice.

Eric is doing his best encourage Anna.

"Well, we all have to start somewhere. What if one day I bring my bass or keyboard and we jam a little?"

Anna tries to hide her excitement. "Well, I'm not that good."

Janeane interrupts the two.

"Foods ready guys. I made pork chops, rice and salad."

Anna gets up and asks to be excused.

"Ma, I told grandpa I would eat with him. He's taking me for ice cream too."

Janeane looks a little disappointed. "It's ok. I'll wrap up the food for lunch tomorrow."

Janeane puts down the plate and hugs Anna, giving her daughter a kiss on the forehead.

"Behave for your grandfather. Love you."

Anna smiles "I will. Love you to Ma."

Anna is about to run out the door and stops to say good bye to Eric. "Bye. Nice to meet you."

Anna heads out the door and closes it behind her. Janeane walks over towards Eric with two plates of food. There is a look of shocked on her face. "Wow!!!! That was huge!!!!"

Smiling, Eric says. "What was?"

Janeane hands Eric his plate and she sits across from him on the couch. "My daughter is never that talkative to men."

He smiles. "I told you kids like me."

Janeane's face glows. "You are a powerful man."

Eric snaps his fingers. "What can I say? If I was gay, I would date me."

Janeane laughs. "You really are too much."

"So.... Tell me more about yourself.

Janeane avoids eye contact.

"Not much too tell. Growing up was never easy. My parents and I never really got along. I used writing as a means to escape. Sadly, I haven't done enough of that these days. After my dad left. My mother and I had some issues. I left my house at fifteen. I moved in with my first boyfriend. He was very controlling. So, I left. Then I met Anna's father. He was a family friend."

Eric softly speaks.

"Fifteen? That's a hard age to leave home. How old was Anna's father?"

Janeane avoids eye contact.

"Thirty-three. He was chasing me for years and I gave in. He was always kind to me. That was until I moved in with him. It was better than staying in my mother's house. He felt I had to be taken care of. Then he kept throwing things in my face. Things like me going to school and trying to blame me for getting pregnant. He took all my journals and burned them. That was the last straw for me. The only thing about him I don't regret is having Anna. The last ex....I won't even get into that."

Eric holds her hand. "That good huh?"

They both chuckle.

"Let's just say that I never had good judgment with men. How about you? No kids. Single. Who are you?... How did you get to be a jingle writer?"

Eric starts to laugh.

"I had my share of bad relationships but I always wanted a family. Not just a kid whose mother I wouldn't get along with. As for the jingle writing. That was not by choice, I can tell you that."

Janeane makes the horns with her hands.

"Let me guess. You were in a rock band."

Eric chuckles. "Nope! A boy band."

Janeane looks at Eric. "Come on! No way!!"

Eric smiles.

"Kidding. We were gonna take over the world. Sadly, ego and drugs got in the way. I got an offer from a company to write the theme song for a wrestler. That paid the bills and the rest as they say is history."

Janeane nods her head.

"Have you ever thought about going back to it?"

Eric ponders. "Maybe, but right now I enjoy eating. As for my parents, they are wacky. We never really got along. I am sure they get mad because I forget to visit and call. "

Concern grows on Janeane's face.

"You sure you got room for me? I don't want to be another project."

Eric takes her by the hand and lifts her face with his other hand. "Janeane, please never think that. You would never be a project. In love, you make time for those you want to be with. I want to be with you."

She smiles and he kisses her passionately.

Chapter 7

Janeane is baking while Anna licks the bowl of batter. "Stop that, you're not a puppy."

Anna playful barks, Arf, Arf! Ma, I really like Eric! He's so cool! He said one day he'd take us to his studio and I could record some music.

Janeane smiles.

"I'm so happy you are happy.' Anna's still licking the bowl.

"Why are you making a cake? Is it Eric's birthday?"

Janeane pulls out cake pans from the oven. "It's now a year since Eric and I have been dating. I thought it would be a nice surprise."

Anna giggles.

"What's so funny, young lady?"

Anna continues to giggle.

"You celebrate everything."

Janeane puts icing on the tip of Anna's nose.

"Ok, wise guy help me. It's movie night and Eric will be over soon."

Later that night Eric, Janeane and Anna are watching a movie. Janeane gets up to use the bathroom.

"Guys, can I pause this? I gotta go to the bathroom."

Anna whines.

"Ma, this is the best part."

Janeane's legs start to shake.

"I been holding it long enough."

Eric pauses the movie.

"Let her go before she makes a mess on the floor."

Anna and Eric chuckle.

Janeane runs to the bathroom. Eric leans over to make sure the coast is clear, he then faces Anna.

"Anna, can I ask you something?"

Anna whispers.

"Sure. Whas' up?"

Eric pulls a small box out of his pocket, opens it and shows Anna a two-point carat heart-shaped engagement ring.

"It's been a year so far and I would like to ask your mother to marry me. However, I would love your permission."

Anna grows uncomfortable.

"NO!!! I have a father already. I don't need another one."

Anna gets up and walks to her room.

Janeane walks back in the room and hears Anna's door slam. Janeane looks at Eric.

"What happened to Anna?"

Eric is not sure what to say.

"She went to her room, one of her friends called her."

Janeane has a puzzled look on her face.

"What the freak? She loves this movie."

Janeane sits next to Eric

"MMmm, this gives us alone time."

Chapter 8

The next morning Janeane knocks on Anna's bedroom door.

"Time to wake up, sweetie."

Janeane walks to the kitchen to get breakfast ready for the both of them. She calls out to Anna.

"Anna, come on! I got a lot to do today."

Anna walks into the kitchen with her head down. Janeane looks over at Anna and senses that her daughter is upset.

"What's wrong, doll?"

Anna sits down and remains quiet.

Janeane ask again.

"What's going on my love?"

Anna still not uttering a word. Janeane grows more concerned, her daughter is never this tight lipped with her.

"Talk to me, my love."

Anna avoids eye contact with her mother and speaks softly.

"I don't like Eric, Ma. I liked it better when it was just us."

Janeane sits down next to Anna.

"Why? You guys were getting along just fine."

Anna's voice gets a little shakey.

" I don't want him here!! I want it to be just you and me. Like before! You promised!"

Janeane grows perplexed by Anna's change in attitude.

"Come on Anna, let's not keep going over this. He's a good man and he cares for you a lot. Why are you so upset? What happened?"

Anna's eyes well up with tears. She gets up and shouts!

"JUST RESPECT OUR OATH!!"

Janeane gets up.

"You better control that funky attitude. This is sudden, after all that we have been doing together, for a year, now you hate him?"

Anna yells. "BECAUSE!"

As Anna starts to cry, a worried expression grows on Janeane's face.

"Because, what? Anna I can't fix things if you don't talk to me."

Anna breaks down crying and replies in a shaky voice.

"Because, he wants to marry you!!!"

Janeane's face lights up. "He told you that?"

Anna whispers between the tears in her eyes.

"He asked my permission."

More curious now, Janeane asks, "What did you say?"

Anna wipes streaming tears from her face.

"No! I don't want you to get married, Ma. We don't need him. Please, don't do it!"

Janeane walks over to Anna hugs her and plays with her hair, attempting to console her

"Baby, let me think about it. Okay? Besides, he may not ask now knowing that you are upset. He respects you and likes you a lot."

Anna remains upset, but explains her logic.

"I don't want him in my life like that, Ma. I have a father. I like him, but he's not my father."

Janeane gently holds Anna by the chin so they can look one another in the eyes.

"He doesn't wanna take your father's place, but he does love us very much and is always thinking of us."

Anna's eyes are red from crying and rubbing.

"I do like him. I just don't want to get use to him and have him leave us too."

Janeane kisses Anna's forehead.

"I know, you've been hurt before and I blame myself. Something tells me, he'll stick around for a long time. Don't worry so much, about the past, things will work themselves out. I gotta finish getting ready."

Anna storms out of the room as Janeane thanks a deep breath and starts to cry. She slowly picks up the phone to call Eric. "Hey, listen, my daughter is very upset and I think we need to take a break. I am sorry. I know that I keep doing this to you, but I just can't do this right now. I know you must hate me; however, I have to think of my daughter first. I do love you, but I have to say Good-bye. "

Janeane hangs up the phone puts her hands over her face and starts to cry. Anna, who has moved closer to the kitchen in order to hear the conversation, slowly walks over to where her mother is sitting. She hugs her mother.

"It's gonna be okay, Ma. I promise."

Janeane gets up and walks out of the room. Anna takes a seat and sees her mother's cell phone. She picks it up to dial Eric's number and looks around to make sure her mother is not nearby.

She speaks softly into the receiver.

"Okay, you can marry her, but you better not hurt her. Promise me! Hold on..."

Anna calls out to her mother.

"Ma!!! Come here quick. grandpa wants to talk to you."

Janeane shouts from the room. "I don't wanna talk right now."

Anna thinks for a moment and then shouts for her mother again.

"Ma, come here, please. Now grandma's on the phone. She needs you badly."

Janeane shouts back from the room.

"I said, I don't wanna talk right now!"

Anna rolls her eyes as frustration rises.

"Geezz Eric! She's playing hard to get"

Shouting back to her mother.

"OOOOOUCHHH!!! MA!! MA!! I CUT MY HAND!!! IT'S BLEEDING BAD!! HURRY!!!"

Janeane runs into the kitchen.

"OH MY GOD!! HOW BAD IS IT?........"

Anna hands Janeane the phone. Janeane looks at Anna, perplexed as she reaches to take the phone from her daughter.

"It's Eric! I told him that it's okay for you two to get married."

Anna hugs her mother and walks out of the room. Janeane stunned by her daughter's actions, puts the phone up to her ear. Her eyes are red from crying. "Hi...Please ask me."

On the other end of the phone, Eric proposed.

"Janeane, you truly are all that I ever wanted in a woman and you make my life meaningful. I would love nothing more than to spend my life in your arms, to stare in your eyes and see your love reflecting back at me. Will you do me the honor of being my life, my world, my oxygen, and my wife?"

Janeane starts to cry.

"YES!!! YES!! ANNNNNND YES!!!"

Chapter 9

Eric and Janeane's wedding day arrived. At Janeane's request, it was a small affair held at her father's country club. While checking her dress in the bridal room mirror yet again, Janeane she sees Anna's reflection behind her. Her daughter's skin is glowing and her dress is picture-perfect. Anna looks beautiful.

"Anna."

Anna stops twirling in front of the mirror and regards her mother's shapely silhouette draped in a modest white two-piece silk suit.

"Yes, Ma?"

Janeane fights back her tears.

"You look so beautiful, thank you for giving Eric a chance."

Anna smiles. "I like him. He's silly."

Anna hugs her mother tightly and whispers, "I love you, Mom"

"I love you too, Anna."

Meanwhile, Eric is standing at the alter waiting for his bride to be. There is a small gathering in attendance. Mostly friends from the Black Star and a few of Eric's business acquaintances. Click…Clack…Click… Clack. The priest looks at Eric. Embarrassed by his nervous habit of clicking a tic tac container. Eric mouths an apology. The music commences and Anna, the flower girl, walks down the aisle first. Eric smiles broadly. His mouth is dry and he can feel his eyes begin to moisten. Thinking to himself. I wish I could drink my tears.

The music tempo changes and Janeane launches into the traditional two-step bridal march. Eric's heart beats frantically and tears roll down his cheek. Radiant, the bride-to-be glides down the aisle. As she gets closer, Eric's face beams in anticipation of holding her hand. He notices that tears are streaming down her cheeks as well. What a pair, we are, he remarks to himself.

Janeane looked at Eric as if no one else were in the church. She couldn't believe how in love she was with this man. Her mind racing with love, fear, hope and doubt. She always kept her walls up, constantly waiting for the so-called shoe to drop.

She thought to herself, 'What did all that matter. He loves me and is so great to Anna. We'll be ok." This was the wedding of her dreams and she did not care if it was fancy or not as long as the right man was at the altar – and he was. As Janeane drew closer, she saw Eric's eye's brimming with joyful tears. In spite of her resolve, she can feel emotions beginning to accelerate. She smiles to force back an outburst.

The priest begins. "Both Eric and Janeane have written their own vows. Janeane you may start."

Janeane takes a moment to compose herself and looks directly into Eric's eyes.

"My sweetest love, where to begin? I gave up on love and felt that it would never find me. Yet, here I stand in front of the most beautiful heart I've ever met. You became my friend, my heart, and my champion. From our first kiss, our hearts have beat as one. I am proud to become your partner, your soul mate and your wife."

Eric's inhales deeply at the admission of love and the tenderness of his bride-to-be. His voice shakes a little at the first word but then levels off as he realizes how important this moment is to Janeane.

"Janeane, my life, my air and my reason for living. Love at first sight was something I only heard of until I met you. I dedicate my life to you and Anna. With you in my life, everything has new meaning, even the polluted New York smog I breathe."

Light laughter rises up from the audience.

"You have been everything I hoped for and each day I look into your eyes, I am grateful and honored to have your heart and soul. As your partner and husband, I will do everything in my power to make you and your precious daughter happy."

The priest solemnly looks from Janeane to Eric.

"By the power invested in me, I know pronounce you husband and wife! Eric, you may kiss your bride!"

Eric and Janeane embrace and share their first passionate kiss as husband and wife while family and friends applaud.

Chapter 10

The door swings opens to Janeane's apartment. Back from their honeymoon, Eric and Janeane are standing outside of the door. Eric ceremoniously picks Janeane up and walks into the apartment. Gazing into her eyes, he speaks.

"You make me so happy. I can't believe you're all mine."

Janeane kisses Eric's top and bottom lip tenderly before he continues.

"Baby, you truly are God's gift. Thank you for showing me how to love again."

Janeane carefully works her way down out of Eric's arms, looks around her small apartment, and remarks to herself. This is a drab comparison to those two weeks in the honeymoon suite in Hawaii. But then nothing that wonderful can last forever.

Readjusting to reality, Janeane sets her handbag down on the coffee table before calling out her daughter's name.

"ANNA!!! We're back!"

Anna comes running out of her room and hugs her mother tightly.

"Mom!"

"Hi baby!!! I missed you, my love."

Anna, herself readjusting to the fact that she is a teenager and way too cool to appear to have missed her mother desperately, calms her excitement but continues to hold on to her mother.

"I miss you too, Ma! You looked so tanned."

Anna looks at Eric and gives him a warm smile.

"Hi Eric! You're pretty tanned yourself. How was the honeyyyyyymoon?"
Anna released her mother and wraps her arms around herself to imitate a romantic embrace while making kissing sounds. Janeane and Eric laugh at the dramatic performance of themselves given by Anna.

"Well, little lady, it was great, thank you. And you? No wild parties, right?"
Anna ceases her imitative act, laughs and shakes her head vigorously in to signal that no nonsense has taken place while the adults were away.

Janeane intakes a breath before letting out an audible sigh.

"Okay, back to the real world. I gotta get ready for work tonight."

Anna frowns "Come on! You just got back."

Janeane exaggerates a frown back at Anna.

"I know love. Wanna help me unpack? I need you to help with the presents I picked up for you and your grandparents before you go out. You can tell me all about what you did while I was away. Hopefully, you didn't give your grandfather a hard time."

Anna smirks and gestures a halo over her head. She and Janeane then walk into the bedroom just as Eric's cell phone rings.

"Hello? Who? How did you get this number?

Eric visibly irritated lays down his cell.

"Janeane!! You have a call!"

Janeane walks in and motions to Eric's cell with a puzzled look on her face. Eric whispers in response, "Anna's father."

Janeane picks up the cell phone tentatively and holds it against her ear. She experiences a mix of emotions that range from anger through embarrassment. The hesitancy betrays her continued trepidation with regard to her abusive ex. Gathering strength from Eric's presence, she speaks sharply into the cell.

"Who gave you this number? … Don't bother lying. … Anna is dressed and waiting for you to pick her up. WHAT?!!! Come on!! You're always pulling this crap. I have to work tonight! It's not his responsibility! FINE! AS USUAL, I'LL HANDLE IT. Fuck yourself, you selfish asshole!!!"

Janeane presses the END CALL button and hands the cell phone back to Eric. His irritation has been replaced by concern though his expression remains relaxed. As Janeane was speaking with her ex, Eric noticed the color draining from her face and the noticeable shaking in her hands. Although externally angered, it was apparent that the call had drained her emotionally.

He asks gently. "What is it?"

"The same old bullshit. Anna's father acting like an ass. He won't take her, so now I have to miss work."

"Is that all that upset you?"

"Well, no. He also said, 'Tell your new husband to handle it.'"

Eric feels his brow begin to tighten and composes himself before reaching for his new bride. The hug does little to quiet her trembling, yet Janeane's arms remain snuggly around his waist.

"Tell you what… let me stay with Anna. I can pop in a flick. microwave some popcorn and Anna and I can have girl talk. I mean, I learned how living with five sisters."

Janeane tightens the embrace, pulling Eric even closer.

"You sure? You know how she can get. Let me ask her first, okay?"

Eric reaches down and lifts Janeane chin up with one finger. He does not let her go as he reassures her.

"Sure, I mean if I'm gonna be in her life, we're gonna need to get use to one another. Plus, I was raised in a house full of women. So, I think I can relate, some what? Wait, that really doesn't sound good."

The tension in Janeane's body relaxes and she laughs before planting a kiss on Eric's cheek.

"You can always make me laugh. How did I get so lucky?"

Eric chuckles "You call this lucky?"

Janeane playfully slaps Eric. "Shhhh you."

Disengaging from the comfort of Eric's formidable embrace, Janeane braces herself.

"Anna! Come here, sweetie. I need to ask you something."

Anna walks into the kitchen and eyes the two adults. She senses the change in mood and prepares herself.

"What?"

Janeane corrects her daughter. "It's yes, not what?"

Anna huffs. "Yes, Mooooommmm..."

Janeane hated to be the one with the news of yet another broken promise. "Your father is not taking you tonight."

Anna sighs. "Again, why?"

Anna eyes start to well up with tears. Janeane reaches for her daughter. Anna does not fight the embrace but instead collapses into her mother's arms.

"Why does he always do this? I always behave when we are together. I never bother him and I try not to ask him for anything."

Janeane is both saddened and angry at her ex for consistently disappointing their daughter.

"I know my love. It's not your fault. You're an amazing daughter."

Anna wipes away the tears that have streamed down her cheek.

"I don't feel like that Mom. I feel like he doesn't even want me."

Janeane draws her daughter closer and presses a kiss onto the top of her head.

"I am so sorry, baby. Listen, I love you more than life itself. I will always be here. Haven't I been your mommy and daddy for all these years? I can stay home with you, if you like."

Anna shakes her head as she withdraws from her mother's embrace.

"No, Ma. I'll be okay. I just want to go to sleep."

Janeane sighs, almost on the verge of tears herself, witnessing the damage done to her Anna's self-esteem. Pulling herself up to full height, she draws Eric in from the periphery where he has been watching his first domestic drama unfold. Unsure of what to do, Eric knows that he will do whatever he can, to prevent anymore hurt to his new wife and step-daughter.

"Eric will stay with you, Anna. Maybe you two can watch a movie or something."

Eric chimes in. "I'll even let you pick out the movie. Within reason of course."

Several stressful moments pass as Janeane and Eric await Anna's response. To their relief, she opens the cabinet over the counter and pulls down a package of microwavable popcorn. Tossing the package to Eric, she feigns a commanding tone. "I pick, you pop."

"Copy that," replies Eric, as he gestures a comical salute.

Chapter 11

Janeane, Sabrina, and Lillian hang decorations for Cinco de Mayo, covering the coffee shop with Mexican motifs. Sabrina performs a little solo dance number to the Latin music streaming from the cook's radio while Janeane reaches for a broom. Lillian rolls a trash bin over toward the end of the counter and says in her characteristic booming voice.

"Soooooooo… Chica…Details!!!"""

Janeane giggles. "Shut up! I don't kiss and tell." Lillian shoots you kidding me look.

"Yeah, and?…" They all laugh. Janeane takes a sip of her coffee.

"Well, we stayed at one of his uncles places in Hawaii. It was sooooooo amazing. It really felt like a movie."

Lillian playfully replies.

"Hawaii? Shhhhhhiiitttt. All I got was dying gas station roses for my honeymoon."

Sabrina laughs and one ups Lillian. "What?… I got a two-pump chump. He was like boom, boom and snore." They all giggle. Janeane continues to talk about the trip.

"We did so many great things and he's been so amazing. It scares the hell out of me."

Curiously Sabrina asked "How so? I mean the man is all about you."

Janeane continues her thought. "I know, but real love is huge. I don't even think I'm good enough for him. He is so sweet and attentive." Sabrina waits for a pause to Janeane's observation.

"No, I get it. Real, true love is scary. But you two are embracing it. Just be honest and real with one another."

Janeane exhales. "I know, but I am always waiting for something f'ed up to happen and he hasn't done anything. I can't believe how much we get along and how thoughtful he is. Half the time I wanna run from him, the other times I wanna freeze the moment."

Sabrina tries to ease her friends mind. "Look, you threw him away and he came back. Your daughter threw him away and he came back. Lets face it, that motherfucker's a boomerang."

Lillian noticed Janeane looks a little flushed. "You ok gurl?"

Janeane is looking around. "No, I have been feeling like crap since last week."

Janeane turns and throws up in the trash can. Both waitress look shockingly at one another and with her booming voice, Lillian almost shouts.

"OH SHIIIIITTTTT!!!! You got knocked up!!! Christmas and Eric cums early!"

Janeane straightens up with a stunned look on her face. Sabrina chuckles. "I knew you had a glow, but I thought it was newlywed memories."

Janeane's face goes pale, even the blood from her lips seemed to have left. Her mind begins to race as a flood of questions pour out of Janeane's mouth.

"Oh no! This is not good. What if he's not ready for a baby? What if I'm not? Anna...."

Sabrina giggles. "Don't jump the gun gurl. We are just fucking with you."

Lillian had to pepper Sabrina's statement. "Yeah, though you may wanna get a test on the way home."

Janeane bites her bottom lip. Memories of her last pregnancy with Anna was the happiest she's ever been before meeting Eric. She places her hands on her belly and smiles about the possibility.

Janeane walks in from her shift at the coffee shop. She sees Eric making breakfast. Eric turns and smiles.

"Morning beautiful girl, you are just in time. Anna is getting ready for school. Her lunch is ready and I'm working on breakfast." Janeane whispers. "I'll be right back. Gotta use the bathroom."

Janeane runs to the bathroom. Eric shrugs his shoulders and continues cooking. He shouts out.

"Ooookkk. Anna breakfast is ready."

Anna runs into the kitchen and grabs a seat.

"I heard the door, was that mom?"

Eric setting up Anna's plate. "Yeah, guess she had to poop."

They both giggle. Janeane walks out to the bedroom, holding her stomach.

"Love's, I'm going to bed. I don't feel well. Anna, please bring me my bag."

Anna gets up from the table and grabs the bag and walks towards the bedroom.

Janeane is laying on the bed, she looks pale.

"Ma! You ok?

Janeane kisses Anna's hand.

"Yes, my love. Just something I ate. How did it go last night?"

Anna sits next to her mother and caresses her hair.

"Good. He let me watch some girlie movies and we talked about you."

Janeane puts on a playful angry face.

"Talked about me? Hmm, it better have been good."

Anna smiles while playing with her mother's hair.

"Don't worry, it was."

Anna gets up. "I gotta run to school. I love you ma!"

Janeane points to her cheek. Anna gives her a kiss.

"Love you too, have a good day."

Anna leaves the room. She walks by the kitchen.

"Eric, watch my mom, she's not feeling so hot."

Eric turns and faces Anna

"Sure thing. Here I made you an egg sandwich to eat on the way. Also, don't forget we gotta go shopping after school."

Anna smiles. "Ok"

Eric walks to the bedroom. Sees Janeane crying.

"Hey, you ok?"

Janeane turns to him.

"Can you lay next to me and hold me?"

Eric lays down and spoons with her. Janeane bites her bottom lip, lets out a sigh and ask Eric.

"Why do you love me?"

Eric stun by the question. "Huh? What makes you ask that?"

Janeane playfully nudges Eric

"Tell me why?"

Eric kisses her on her ear lobe.

"How can I describe love? When I first laid eyes on you my stomach was in knots. My heart would pound so loud, I thought you could hear it. Then getting to know you and who you really are, was amazing to me. You make me feel like I'm superman and there is nothing we can't do. When you broke up with me. I felt like a lost child in the dark, reaching out for your hand. You have been the best thing that ever happened to me. This is the life I always envisioned."

Janeane turns to face Eric.

"Good answer. How'd you get so smart?"

Eric looks Janeane in the eyes

"I can't imagine a life where you and I are apart. Which is what I wanted to talk to you about. I know you are a strong and independent woman, but I don't want you to work anymore. Now, before you say no, hear me out, ok? You're a writer, it's time you start writing."

Janeane smiles.

"Thank you, baby, but there's no money in writing. Which is why I'm at the coffee shop."

Eric continues to try and convince Janeane.

"I'd rather you work on what makes you happy. That's not your life, please let me help. Besides, we just locked in the football account. Please, give me that gift."

Janeane lays her hand on his face while looking him in the eyes.

"I already got you a gift."

Janeane takes Eric's hand and places it on her stomach. Eric's eyes well up.

"You mean...a baby?"

Janeane nobs her head.

"Yes! You're gonna be a father. You don't hate me, right?"

Eric smiles and tears roll down his cheek. He hugs Janeane.

"Wow! Baby!! This is amazing!!"

Janeane kisses Eric on the lips.

"Don't say anything to Anna yet, I don't know how to tell her."

Eric still has a big Kool aid smile on his face.

"You got it. When did you know?"

Janeane looking at the twinkle in Eric's eyes.

"Last night. I was scared to tell you, but I can see the look in your eyes. I can see your happiness."

They go back to the spooning position. Eric thinking.

"What will we name it?"

Janeane giggles. "It? Her, we'll name her Layla."

Eric puzzled questions the name choice.

"Layla? Why that name?"

Janeane blushes a little. "It was the song that played when I first met you."

Eric kisses Janeane deeply."

Chapter 12

Anna walks in the door. Janeane is sitting on the chaise. Anna walks over to her mother and kisses her on the cheeks.

"How are you feeling ma?"

Janeane taps on the chaise.

"Better my love. Come sit next to me."

Anna takes a seat.

"How was school?" Anna flops on the chase.

"Long and boring, but there was some kind of crazy food fight during lunch. They started throwing food and cursing."

Janeane "Did you get hit with any food?"

Anna shakes her head side to side.

"Noooooo, I stayed under the table."

They both giggle. Janeane looks at Anna.

"You ok with me being married? Are you happy with him?"

Anna nods. "He's growing on me. At least he's around and wants me around. Are you ok ma?"

Janeane holds Anna's hand.

"Yes, my love. I just wanted to make sure you were ok with all that has happened."

Anna sighs

"It's not easy, but he has been nice to both of us. He's better than the last guy."

Janeane takes a deep breath.

"I don't know how else to tell you this?"

Anna over reacts.

"YOU GUYS ARE SPLITTING UP?!!!! I KNEW IT!! WHY EVEN BOTHER!!!"

She stops Anna's rant. "No, no, no! Think of some other surprise. A good one."

Anna looks up. "Hmm, yoooooouuuuuu won the lotto?"

Janeane giggles. "I wish!"

Anna starts looking around the room. "Hmm, You bought me a puppy?"

Janeane shoots that one down. "No silly."

Anna starts to get inpatient.

"Just tell me!!"

Janeane feels a little nervous on breaking the news.

"How would you feel about being a big sister?" Anna seems a little upset.

"Already?... Really, ma?"

Janeane tries to comfort her daughter.

"It wasn't planned baby, but yes."

Anna has a look of disappointment.

"Great. Now I'll never have you to myself, ever again."

Janeane kisses Anna's hand. "No, mi armor. You will always have me, but for the next few months you'll have a lot more of me around."

Anna puffs up her cheeks. "Why, because you're gonna get fat?"

Janeane gives her a playful angry look.

"What?!"

They both laugh.

"No!!!! Silly, I am going to be working from home. I'm gonna work on my writing."

Anna is excited at the idea of more time with her mother. "Wow, so I'll see you all night? No more working late? Umm, does my dad know about the baby?"

Janeane takes a sip of coffee. "No, I told Eric and then you. Your father can wait to hear this news."

Anna knowing her father all too well. "He won't be happy."

Knowing Anna is right. "I'll deal with him, just not today."

As months go by, Eric and Janeane look for new places to live. Buying baby clothing and accessories. They go in for Janeane's check. The doctor invites Eric in.

"Sir, you may accompany your wife."

Eric gets up and walks into the room with Janeane. The doctor places the gel on Janeane's belly and begins the sonogram.

"Would like the know the sex of the baby?"

Eric and Janeane look at one another. They both agree.

"YES!"

The doctor moves the wand.

"If you both can look at the screen you will see. It's a girl!"

Janeane shouts in excitement.

"YAY! Sorry."

Eric and the doctor laugh. Eric looks at Janeane. "How did you know it was gonna be a girl?"

Janeane smiles at Eric "Lucky guess."

The day of the new baby finally arrives. A new loft style apt with Christmas decorations still up. Anna is hanging welcome home signs and a few other family members are standing around, waiting for Janeane and Eric to come home from the hospital. Anna hears the keys in the door and she shhh's everyone.

"Turn off the lights!!"

The door opens, Janeane has the a new born in her arms. Eric has all sorts of bags in his hands. Everyone shouts softly.

"SURPRISE!!!"

Everyone crowds around Janeane and the baby. A look of happiness falls on the face of Eric and Janeane. Anna runs over to play with her baby sister. Late that night everyone has gone home and Eric is cleaning up. Janeane

and Anna are on the chase with the baby. Anna gets up and offers to help Eric.

"Thank you, Anna, but I got it. Spend some time with your mother and sister. Anna smiles. "OK!"

The morning comes and it's back to normal life for both Eric and Anna. Eric kisses both Janeane and baby Layla on the forehead.

"I gotta run. Please text me if you need me."

Anna comes and also sneaks in a kiss to Janeane and Layla.

"Bye little sister. Be good for mommy. Bye ma, love you."

Janeane lays in bed exhausted and has no drive. Janeane forces herself up and walks into the room and sits on her chaise. Layla is in her crib. Layla begins to cry. Janeane doesn't move from her spot. As if she does not hear the crying baby. She sits there with a blank stare on her face. This goes on all day. Suddenly she is snapped out of it by the sound of keys. The door opens and in walks Anna. Janeane jumps up and runs to get the baby. She walks over and sits on a chase with the baby in her arms. Anna kneels next to her mother. "Wow, ma, She's so tiny. She looks like a doll."

Janeane forces a smile.

"You were like this once, now you're freaking taller than me. You wanna hold your sister?"

Anna nods an exciting yes.

"Ok, just make sure you support her head ok?"

Anna looks at her mother with the playful angry face they use with one another.

"I have held a baby before ma. Hello, baby sitter here. Give me my sister."

Janeane hands the baby to Anna. Janeane exhales

"Good, now I can rest. Do you know if Eric is in the downtown studio?"

Anna baby talking to Layla.

"Yeah, he is working on that big job for the football ads."

Janeane grabs her phone. "I'll text him to bring milk and diapers." Anna is baby talking to her sister.

An hour later Eric walks into the loft. His face lights up as he sees the girls in the living room.

"What man is luckier than me? A home with a Queen and two princesses. Anna want me to take the baby?"

Anna shakes her head no. "I just got her."

Eric turns to Janeane

"Hey, You ok? You look so tired."

Janeane has tears in her eyes. She seems distant. Eric Ask again "Janeane, are you ok?"

Janeane snaps out of her daze.

"Yeah, just a little beat. The baby wasn't feeling too well and I was getting into it with my dad. He's upset that I haven't made it a point to go see him."

Eric sits by the chaise where Janeane is laying down.

"Sorry, to hear that. Do you want me to take Anna and the baby to see him?"

Janeane starts sobbing. "Eh, let me think about it. I really don't wanna talk about it now."

Eric playing with Janeane's hair as he knows that soothes her.

"OK."

Anna chimes in. "Ma, we should go. He's been blowing up my phone."

Janeane snaps at Anna.

"I said let me think about it! OK!"

Anna is visibly upset by her mother's reaction gets up and gives Layla to Eric.

"I'm going to my room."

Eric is taken aback by Janeane's outburst. "Aww baby, you shouldn't have went off like that."

Janeane looks upset. "I know, just so tired, I haven't been able to write or even think. I can't have everyone pulling at me."

Eric looks her in the eyes. "Let me know what you need help with. We are a team, remember?"

Janeane wipes the mist from her eyes. "Sorry, I've just been cranky. Anyway, how's work going?"

Eric leans over and kisses Janeane on the forehead. "It's ok. As for work, it's a music video for the football commercial, those people are a pain in my ass! I mean, butt. Sorry my princess."

Janeane laughs "She's too young to understand you."

Eric shrugs his shoulders. "With my luck, her first words will be curse words. If that happens, I'm blaming you."

Janeane gets up and starts to walk to Anna's room.

"Hey love, are you ok?"

Janeane turns to Eric.

"Yeah, just run down I guess. Can you stay with the baby? I wanna apologize to Anna. Maybe get some of my own writing done."

Eric smiles. "Sure thing." Eric looks at the baby.

"You are a powerful child. Only you could bring us all together. I love you."

The next morning, Eric and Anna are heading out the door. Janeane stops them both and kisses them and they head out the door. The baby starts crying. Janeane, begins to cry and sits on the couch. Leaving the baby in the room.

She begins to think out loud.

"I don't understand, why I am not happy? I have a loving man and family. Then why do I feel so alone? I can't feel love...I feel so cold and numb. My head is racing with ugly thoughts about myself, worse about the baby. Half the time I love holding her, she is so beautiful. Some days, I wish she was never here. How can I ever explain that to Eric? I can't, I'll lose him forever. How do I sit him down and say some days...Some days I want to just run away or die? Does this make me a bad person? I just feel so overwhelmed by all this. What's happening to me?"

She starts to sob, Janeane Looks up.

"I know, I know I'll start writing."

She quickly grabs her note pad and a pen. The baby starts to cry louder and louder. Janeane is frustration lets out a scream and throws her coffee cup across the room. She gets up and is over the crib. She takes a pillow in her hand. the look in her eyes are cold and blank. she slowly moves the pillow towards the baby. She suddenly snaps out of it. she falls to her knees crying. *"I'm sorry, I'm sorry...I'm sorry. Oh my god...what the fuck is wrong with me?"*

Chapter 13

Later that evening, Eric walks in the front door. The aroma of his favorite dish greets him at the door. Anna is playing with the baby and Janeane is preparing the food. Suddenly Janeane lets out a scream. She comes running out with a hand towel soaked in blood over her hand. Eric jumps up.

OH MY GOD, WHAT HAPPENED?"

Janeane snaps at Eric.

"WHAT DO YOU THINK? YOU SEE BLOOD RIGHT?"

A shocked expression falls on his face, as he stumbles on his words.

"Umm, I'm sorry, just was a little shocked. Let me get see how bad it is."

Janeane's eyes almost seem black with anger.

"For what? You can't fix this?! I'll be fine, just leave me alone. I can't get any peace. FUCK!!"

Janeane storms out the room. Eric has a confused by her outburst, Anna looks upset.

"Anna, did anything happen today?"

Anna has a look of fear on her face, her mother never flips out like this.

"I came home and she was crying on the couch. The baby wasn't changed. She has a little rash, but I put cream on her."

Eric has a look of confusion on his face.

"Ok, wonder what happened today?"

Eric knocks on the bedroom door.

"Love are you ok? Do you need to go to the hospital?"
With a clam tone to her voice.
"I'll be just fine, please just let me rest." Eric respects her request and goes to finish cooking the food.

After numerous request by her girlfriends, Janeane agrees to have them over for a visit. As Sabrina and Lillian approach the front door they can hear Janeane singing to Layla, they ring the door bell. Janeane opens the door and smiles as she sees her friends. Lillain looks around at how huge the loft is
"Hey gurl!!! This is nice."
Sabrina agrees
"Really nice."
Janeane laughs.
"Thanks ladies, take a seat. You want coffee?"
Sabrina jokingly interrupts Janeane.
"Excuse me, baby first!"
Janeane walks into the other room to bring out the baby. Both Sabrina and Lillain let out a collective.
"Aww"
Lillian holds out her arms. "She so gorgeous. Let me hold her please." They all sit down. Sabrina notices that Janeane seems off, she's constantly looking off to this distance. She's not her usual bubbly self.
"How have you been? We haven't heard from you in ages."
Lillian adds. "I know, you use to talk to us all the time."
Janeane makes a sad face.
"I know, I suck. It's been really hard with the baby and all. I forgot how much work goes into having a newborn."
Sabrina tries to bring up a happy subject.
"How's the writing going? Still working on the waitress idea? If so we want our cut."

Janeane is starting into space. Sabrina snaps her fingers.

"HEY YOU! Wake up!"

Janeane almost seemed startled.

"I'm sorry, what happened?" Sabrina continues. "I asked how the writing was going?"

Janeane lets out a deep sigh.

"Sucks, I haven't gotten any done. Just been so beat."

Lillian is rocking Layla still in her arms, adds.

"It happens. I was the same way. You just have to adjust."

Janeane looking perplexed.

"I guess, I never really felt like this with Anna. It's really odd. I just feel so off."

Lillain follows up. "Like how?"

Janeane shrugs her shoulders.

"I wish I knew. I been snapping at everyone."

Sabrina notice a bandage around Janeane's wrist. With a concerning tone, she ask.

"What happen to your wrist?"

Janeane a little off put by the question. Her eyes scan the room, before she can answer.

"Stupid me, I was…cooking and I put the knife upside in the drying rack and when I went to reach for something, it cut me. Still hurts like hell."

The room falls silent for a second. Lillian breaks the tension.

"Oh, remember the busboy? The weird looking one? Guess what he got caught doing?"

Sabrina giggles.

"OHHH MY GOD… you gonna tell that story?"

They both start to laugh. Janeane plays along and pleads.

"Come on, tell me!"

Lillain starts to laugh so hard that Sabrina has to tell the story.

"Let's just say he got caught handling his meat in the walk-in freezer." She makes a jerking off motion. They all start laughing. With a surprise look on her face Janeane is shocked.

"Are you freaking kidding me? That's definitely going in my TV show." Anna Walks into the house, looking a little down. Janeane walks over to her. "What happen my love? Why are you here? Your father said he was taking you to eat."

Anna stands on the other side of the room. Waves at Lillain and Sabrina. "Nope! I waited and waited. He text me and told me to go home."

Anna starts to cry and runs to her room. The girls motion to one another to leave. Lillain hugs Janeane and hands her the baby.

"Hey Chica, we're gonna head out."

Janeane knows she has to attend to Anna.

"Ok, sorry ladies. I promise to keep in touch more."

Sabrina looks at Janeane.

"If you need anything, even a baby sitter so you can rest. Just let me know." She leans in and gives Janeane a big hug.

Later that night Eric gets home, he seems a little bothered. He walks over to Janeane and kisses her on the lips.

"Hey baby, how was your day? Janeane hugs Eric by the neck. "It was ok, Anna's father blew her off again. I hate that he does that to her. She cried most of the night. How was your day? You look upset." Eric tries to fake a smile. Janeane looks at him. "I know you better than that, mister" Eric takes a deep breath. "I have to work late here in my studio. They made a last-minute change that will force me to rearrange the chorus. I'm sorry." Janeane kisses Eric, "It's ok love, do what you have to." Eric smiles and gets to work. Without realizing the time Eric sits in his studio listening to the playback of the new chorus. Janeane is standing at the door way with the baby in her arms. Eric does not feel her watching him. She has a look of sadness on her face. She walks behind Eric and places her hand on his cheek. He leans into it and kisses her palm. He turns around in his chair to face Janeane and the baby. He notices the baby is sound asleep.

"So, how are my girls doing tonight?"

Janeane whispers

"Ok, Anna's father picked her up and the baby just fell asleep. How's work going handsome?"

Eric stretches "Great, got a lot done. Your timing is perfect, as always."

Janeane leans in and kisses Eric on the forehead.

"You always know what to say."

Eric chuckles and stands up to hug Janeane and the baby.

"Can you do me a favor and watch the baby? I want to soak in the tub. Haven't done that in forever."

Eric takes the baby in his arms.

"Sure, I could use some cuddle time with the wee one."

Eric kisses Janeane, He pauses and takes a deep breath of Janeane's skin.

"God, you always smell so good."

Janeane looks down at the baby and then at Eric.

"Silly man, I love both of you."

Eric smiles. "We love you too." Eric sees sadness in her eyes. "Hey, you ok?"

Janeane nervously avoids eye contact.

" Yeah, just not feeling too well. I think the bath will help."

Eric kisses Janeane, her kiss lingers a bit. Eric double checks.

"Can I get you anything?"

Janeane forces a smile. "No, my love I'll be fine. Don't wake up the baby, I just got her down."

Janeane walks out of the room. Eric walks to the living room and sits on the couch, resting the baby on his chest. Shortly after he falls asleep. He is suddenly awaken by the baby crying, the cry sounded so painful. Startled he gets up and tries to get the baby to stop crying. The baby won't stop crying. Eric talks to Layla as if she can understand him.

"Ok, ok, let's find mommy to help me here."

Eric walks to the bedroom, she is not there. He walks to the home office and she is not there. Eric begins to call for her.

"Baby? A little help here, please!"

No answer. He places the baby in the crib, Layla still crying and getting louder. He notices the bathroom door is still closed. He walks over and gentle knocks.

No answer. He tires the door knob and it's not locked. He opens the door.

"Baby, you been in here for a while. I passed out and lost track of the..."

He sees that she is not moving or replying. His voice gets shaky. "Baby, did you fall asleep?"

He notices she is not responsive and not breathing.

"Janeane? Janeane? Come on honey wake up!" He kneels by the bathtub. "No, no, no, noooooo, please wake up?! Please God, No!" He leans in and hugs her lifeless body, He begins to cry. "Please God, please wake up!!!!! Please, please......Oooohhhhh God!"

He struggles to get his cell phone out of his pocket. Refusing to let go of Janeane's body. He begins to cry uncontrollably. The hair on his arms and neck rise! He lets out a yell that would curdle the blood.

"Help! Help! I can't wake her up! Wake up baby, please! Wake up! Help!"

His hands are shaking and he can barely see the screen of the phone through his tears. Suddenly a voice from the other side.

"911 what's your emergency?"

Eric drops the phone and forces out a yell.

"Help my wife! Please! Please!"

Shortly the Paramedics, police and fire department arrive to the scene. Eric is sitting on the toilet, sobbing. The paramedics try to remove Eric from the bathroom. He shows some resistance. The police come and try to talk him out.

"Sir, please you have to come out of there."

One officer takes Eric by the hand. Eric pulls his hand back.

"No! No! She needs me, she needs me to wake her up! Please let me go!... PLEASE!"

One of the officers gets testy.

"Listen! They are here to help. I know this is hard, but I need you to relax. Now!"

Rage builds in Eric eyes as his body shakes.

"You don't know shit! This is my wife! Talk to me when someone you love is dying."

A female officer pushes the rude cop out of the way. She kneels next to Eric.

"Sir, I'm sorry about that. We are all here to help you and your family. Everyone is trying to help your wife. Why don't you take a seat and -"

Suddenly Eric jumps to his feet.

"Where's my baby? Give me my daughter...NOW!"

The female officer tries to calm Eric down.

"Let's go get her. Please try to relax for your daughter."

Another officer walks over and hands Layla to Eric. Eric hugs her. "Mommy's alright baby. Mommy's alright...."

Paramedics calls the officer over. Eric is trying to hear what is being said. The officer walks back to talk to Eric.

"Sir, I am sorry. They couldn't save her. Seems she took a bottle of pills some time ago. We are gonna need to ask you some...."

The officers radio interrupts the conversation.

"We have someone at the door claiming to be the victim's daughter. Please advise"

A look of concern washes over Eric's face.

"Oh no! She wasn't supposed to be home till tomorrow."

Anna begins to yell for her mother.

"MA!... ERIC! What's going on? MA! Mommy!!!"

Eric walks over to Anna, still at the entrance of the house. She sees the sadness on Eric's face. Anna shouts.

"WHAT HAPPENED TO MY MOTHER? MA!.. WHY IS SHE NOT ANSWERING ME?!"

Eric hugs her and starts to cry as he apologizes.

"Anna, I'm... I'm so sorry. I tried to wake her up, I tried…"

Anna breaks free of Eric's hug.

"No! she's not dead, no! Ma! Mommy! Ma!"

Anna runs away. One of the Police officers follow her. Eric is standing at the doorway. A few minutes pass and the officer comes back. "Sir, your step daughter will be staying with her father. In the meantime, we are going to have to ask some questions."

Visibly upset, his face red from crying and tears still rolling down his cheek. Eric looks the officer in the eyes.

"Are you fucking for real? I can't do this shit right now! My Wife is dead, her daughter just found out and my baby is in my hands. Please, leave us alone."

The officer closes his book, leaving his finger in between the pages.

"Sir, I can't begin or pretend to know what you are going through. I just really need to put the pieces together here."

Eric puts his head down

"That makes two of us. I don't get it, you know? We were so happy and now, and now she's gone. Just like that. Why? Why, would she do this to us? All of us!"

The officer looks at Eric with compassion.

"We can do this in the morning. Do you have a place to stay?"

Eric notices that the coroners rolling out the body. Eric begins to cry. The officer puts her hand on his shoulder.

Chapter 14

A few days have passed, Eric's face looks like a man defeated, his smile gone, the twinkle is his eyes have gone dim. He decides to venture back to the loft, shaking and his eyes welling up with tears. Eric slowly walks into the house as if he doesn't belong there. He pauses in the middle, the smell of Janeane's perfume still lingered in house, Eric's chest gets tight, he sees their photos, oh how he loved just looking at his wife and stealing a kiss. Memories of their time together flood his mind, so fast that he can't hold on to one single memory. He falls to his knees he cries a deep painful cry. The kind that knocks the wind out of you, it makes no sound. His tears fall like rain drops during a heavy storm, landing on his lap and soaking his jeans. His soul along with his heart is crushed. He finally lets out a blood curdling yell and begins to cry.

"WHY?!...."

Eric begins to talk as if Janeane was in the room next to him.

"Why? Why would you do this? What did I do? TELL ME!" With rage in his voice he shouts! "WHAT DO I DOOOOO?!"

His sobbing grows harder and harder, as he curls up into a ball, he reaches and grabs a t-shirt she had left on the nearby couch. Hugging it and holding it near his face, so he can smell her one last time. The sobbing is uncontrollable, exhausted from crying he shortly falls asleep. After about an hour he springs up screaming.

"NO! GOD, NO!"

A knock on the door. Confused, Eric slowly gets up off the floor.

"Hello?"

The voice on the other side greets Eric in return.

"Mailman. You have to sign for this delivery."

Eric opens the door slowly.

"Eric Bisley? Please sign here." The mail man hands Eric an envelope.
Eric noticed the address is in Janeane's handwriting. He quickly signs the
form and closes the door. Looking confused he rips open the envelope,
inside there are three smaller envelopes. One with his name, the other
with Anna's name the last with Layla's name. All written in Janeane's
handwriting. He quickly opens the one address to him it. It's a note from
Janeane. She sent for him to read upon her death.

"My luv
There is nothing outside of my daughter and our baby, that means more to me than you.
I knew that night we met, that we were meant to be. No man has ever touch my
mind, heart and soul the way you have.
Little did you know that my inner demons force me to make such horrible mistakes.
The greatest gift you ever gave me was showing me how to love again. I know that the
greatest gift I could give you is Layla. It pains me to know that I am breaking your heart
and the tears you are shedding are from deep in your soul. You've been more than I feel
I deserve. When we met, I saw sadness in your eyes, little did I know I saw the future
and I would be the reason for your sadness. Sadly, I have to go. I can't do this anymore,
I tried love. Life for me has always been a struggle. I will be here watching and loving
you all. Your silent cheerleader. I love you all so very much and I am so sorry. One day,
I will find you my love.
Your Queen Janeane.

Eric stunned by what he just read. He walks over to the couch and sits
down. His cell phone rings.

"Hello?"

On the line its Anna's father.

"Eric?"

Eric still in shock, this is the last voice he wanted to hear.

"Yes, what can I do for you?"

Anna's father talks to Eric in a very matter of fact tone.

"Look, I know you are going through a lot right now, but when can Anna stop by the house?"

Eric concerned as he has not seen Anna since the funeral.

"How is she holding up?"

As if the question was annoying, he replies.

"Hell if I know! It's easier to teach wood to read than to get her to talk. Listen, I'm a very busy man and have a lot to do. Do you think you can take care of her? I'll try to keep up with the usual visit. I just got some major deals to finish up and I can't do that and watch her too."

Eric has a surprised look on his face.

"What? Are you serious? I can't tell you how to raise Anna, but she already lost her mother and you haven't exactly been in the picture."

Anna's father starts to shout.

"HEY! I DON'T NEED YOU TELLING ME ABOUT MY OWN DAUGHTER. I JUST THINK IT WOULD BE EASIER FOR HER TO BE AROUND YOU AND THE BABY IN THAT HOUSE. HER MOTHER WAS SELFISH AND ALWAYS HAS BEEN. SHE CAN EITHER STAY WITH YOU OR HER GRANDFATHER! CALL ME LATER WITH AN ANSWER. I GOTTA GO TO WORK TONIGHT!"

Angry Eric yells back!

"LISTEN ASSHOLE! I LOST MY WIFE AND THE MOTHER OF OUR CHILDREN! YOU WANNA PLAY GAMES? I WILL BE DAMN SURE TO FIGHT FOR CUSTODY OF ANNA! YOU PIECE OF SHIT!"

Silence grows on the other side. Eric hears him take a breath. Suddenly Anna's father speaks.

"There wouldn't be a fight. I have a new life and you may be doing me a favor."

Stunned by his response, Eric was about to talk when the line goes dead. "Hello? Hello?"

Eric looks at his phone.

"What a dildo."

Eric's cell phone rings again. It's his mother.

"Hey ma." Concerned about Eric's emotions. "Hi, are you ok?"

Eric takes a deep breath.

"Yeah...no, I'm just confused. Still taking it day by day. How's the baby?"

She hears his pain.

"I am so sorry son. Layla is ok, you just dropped her off this morning. Why don't you give me some time with my granddaughter?"

Eric lets out a sigh.

"Thanks, but I'll be ok. I need her more than she needs me."

She doesn't push the subject.

"Ok, but don't come by too late, I don't want you waking her up."

Eric with no energy in his voice.

"I won't, I gotta get some stuff done and I'll see you in a few."

Eric hangs up and looks around. He whispers.

"God, I miss you......"

The next day Eric returns with Layla to the loft. Sitting on the couch showing Layla photos of Janeane.

"This is your mommy. See her beautiful smile. She would light up the room."

Suddenly the doorbell rings. Eric gets up to answer the door and see's Anna standing there her eyes red from crying, a duffel bags at her feet. Eric not sure what to say.

"Hi" Anna standing there with a scared look on her face. Eric tries to talk to Anna. "Are you scared to come in?"

Anna nods her head yes. Eric trying to think of a way to make it easier. "How about we grab a bite to eat and come back here when you are ready."

Anna lowers her head. Eric see's Anna's pain.

"I'll take that as a yes. Let me bring your bags in and dress your sister." Anna peeps inside the house and begins to cry. Eric hearing this. He places the baby in the crib and comes back into the room and walks over to Anna. He tries to hug and comfort her, but she pulls away. Rage fills her eyes and her voice start to shake.

"I HATE YOU! THIS ALL YOUR FAULT! WE WERE FINE, JUST FINE! I TOLD HER WE DIDN'T NEED YOU AND THAT BABY AND THIS HOUSE! WE WERE HAPPY! I CAN'T STAND YOU! YOU SHOULD HAVE BEEN THE ONE TO DIE!"

Eric was shocked and sadden by this outburst.

"Anna, know that I am also hurt and sad. She left me too and I love both you so much. Your sister was never a plan, I know you're hurt, I wish I could turn back time and make this all go away. I need you, I need you to help your sister get to know her mother as well."

Anna still crying "Why did she do this?" Eric reaches in his back pocket and pulls out the envelope addressed to Anna.

"I have something for you. I was gonna wait to give it to you. Your mother was not well and I wish I saw this. Please take a seat and if you still wanna hate me then fine, but please don't hate your sister. Like yourself, she is innocent in all this."

Anna puts her head down and whispers.

"I don't wanna come in, please don't make me. Can I just stand right here?"

Eric nods in agreement.

"Ok, please stay here while I get something."

Eric walks across the room and grabs a chair. He brings it over too

Anna. She accepts the chair.

"Thank you. I'm sorry, I don't wish you were dead." Anna takes a seat.

"Your mother left one for each of us. I didn't read it because It's not my place.

You don't have to read this now or even here. The choice is yours."

Tears rolling down both of their faces. Anna still looking down ask for permission to come in.

"Can I come in? It's getting cold."

He picks up her bag.

"Anna, this is your house as well. Please come in. I am going to feed the baby. Can I get you anything?"

Anna walks over to the couch and sits on the edge.

"A Coke, please?"

Eric walks over to the kitchen and grabs a Coke out of the fridge. Hands it to Anna.

"Thank you."

Eric places his hand on Anna's shoulders.

"I am sorry Anna, from the bottom of my heart, I am sorry. You gonna be ok while I feed Layla?"

Anna holding the letter in her hands, her tears tapping the envelope as they fall. She avoids eye contact.

"I guess."

Eric walks out the room. Anna lets out a huge cry.

"NOT FAIR! THIS IS SO NOT FAIR!"

Anna cries for a bit and slowly opens the letter from her mother.

"My sweetest angel.
I know you are in pain and I left with so many questions.
I can try to explain it, but words on paper cannot express true and raw emotions.
I lived my life for you. When you were born nothing else in this world mattered.
All my life I have been in pain and so unhappy and it's not your fault. This
has to do with my own demons and my past. You are such a smart young lady
and I am so proud of you. You are already smarter than I was at your age. My
heart hurts as I will not see you grow into the powerful woman I see in your eyes.
Watch over your sister and be kind to your step father as he loves you like you are
his own. Your sister is a gift to you both. You three are the best thing in my life.
The only rainbows in my dark world. Take care of Layla for me, promise me.
Love you always mi amor.
Mommy"

Chapter 15

Anna begins to cry uncontrollably. Eric is standing at the door. Unsure of how to approach her. He starts to cry as he walks over to Anna. "Looks like we both could use a hug."

Anna hugs Eric. "If she loved me, then why did she do this? Why didn't she wanna see me grow up? or get married? No one wants me, Why? I tried to be good, I tried to be smart."

Eric tries to help Anna understand.

"No, no, Anna. This has nothing to do with your behavior. Your mother would brag about you all the time. She is very proud of you."

With a hint of anger in her voice.

"Then why? Why would she do this? Why did she have to go?"

Eric still trying to figure out how to help her. He searches his mind for something to say.

"Anna, I am trying to put together the piece's. I really am. I didn't see this coming. Just never doubt her love for you, please."

Anna walks towards the other side of the room. Her pain becomes rage as her mind races.

"IF SHE LOVED ME, SHE WOULDN'T HAVE LEFT ME, OK! WHAT'S WRONG WITH ME?! NO ONE WANTS ME! NO ONE! I HEARD MY FATHER TALKING TO YOU...HE DOESN'T WANT ME EITHER. I DON'T NEED ANY OF YOU! YOU CAN ALL GO

TOO HELL!"

Anna runs out the house. Eric runs to the door.

"ANNA! PLEASE COME BACK!"

ANNA!

Eric sits on the couch and calls Anna's father and gets a voice mail. "Anna just ran away from here. Please call or text me if she ends up by your place."

Eric hangs up the phone and calls his father in-law.

"Hello, Hank? Anna ran away from home. Is she with you? No? Please call me if you hear anything."

Eric hangs up the phone.

"FUCK! WHY?! Why?! This isn't fair of you! You left us alone. I don't know what to do here? I'm lost without you. Baby I need you..."

Eric goes and dresses the baby and starts to head for the door. To drive around and try to find Anna. As he opens the door there is a police Officer standing there with Anna.

"Good afternoon sir, Are you Eric Bisley?"

A look of fear came over Eric's face.

"Yes"

He sees Anna walking towards the door with the other officer.

"Anna, are you ok?"

Anna stands there in silence. The officer explains the situation.

"We found her in an empty apartment. The landlord knew her, so there will be no charges. Keep a closer eye on her, will you?"

Eric shakes the Policeman's hand.

"Thank you for bringing her home. Sorry for the inconvenience."

Anna walks in and goes straight to her room. The officer looks around the apartment.

"Is everything ok here sir?"

Eric shakes his head.

"I wish I could say yes. See we just lost my wife, her mother. She's angry and hurt. I am sure she meant no harm."

The Policeman almost regretting he asked such a question.

"Sorry for your loss. Just keep an eye on her and she'll come around when she's ready."

He gives Eric his card. If you need anything feel free to call me, we have some great therapist who specialize in bereavement."

Eric takes the card.

"Thank you. I'll keep that in mind. Have a safe night."

Eric locks the door and puts the baby back in her crib. He knocks on Anna's door.

"Hey, you hungry?"

No answer. Eric tries again.

"You wanna talk?"

No answer.

Eric walks over to a photo of his wedding day. He picks it up and lays on the couch. His eyes get blurry from his tears, he beings to cry. Anna slowly opens her door and hears Eric sobbing and talking to himself.

"Why did you leave us? What am I supposed to do? Anna hates me and the baby will never know you. I miss you so fucking much. I'm so scared and alone. How could you do this to us? I'm sorry I couldn't help you."

Tears roll down Anna's face as she witnesses Eric's pain. She slowly closes her door to leave him in peace.

Eric wakes up and hears the baby giggling. He looks around the living room and sees Anna playing with Layla. He gets up from the couch and hides the photo. He wipes the sleep from his eyes.

"Morning girls. Do you want me to take her?"

Anna is smiling for the first time as she plays with Layla.

"No, I got her. All those babysitting jobs paid off."

Eric not sure what to say or do next.

"You want me to make her a bottle?"

Anna making baby sounds with Layla.

"No, I fed and changed her. My Grandfather said he wants to talk to you. Said he'll be here around noon."

Eric feeling a bit relieved.

"Did he say about what?"

Anna shakes her head.

"Nope."

He looks at his watch.

"Oh man, it's almost noon."

As soon as he utters those words, the door bell rings. "Man, isn't this how it always happens?" Eric opens the door. It's his father in-law.

"Hey Hank, come in."

As they enter the living room, Eric politely ask Anna, to take her sister to her room. Anna nods yes. Eric and Hank walk to the kitchen table. Eric starts to pour himself some coffee.

"Coffee?"

Hank nods no. Eric makes himself a cup and sits across from Hank. Eric nervous about what the topic could be, he looks at Hank.

"I'm not sure what to say. So, I'll let you start."

Hanks eyes are bloodshot red.

"Look, I wasn't the best father in the world. For years, I was my daughter's hero. She would follow me everywhere. A real tomboy, that was my Janeane." Hank's eyes well up.

"As a father, you wanna protect your daughter. You do what your parents taught you."

Eric tries to console his father-in-law.

"Hank, this shit is not easy. We do the best that we can, right?" Eric can see that Hank has the weight of the world in his eyes as he begins to confide in Eric.

"I made life for my wife hell. I took to drinking and started to hit her and drove a wedge between my baby. She never looked at me the same again. She had hate for me. I can't blame her. I failed her.

One day she witnessed me hurting her mother. So, I left. Her mother took up with a man who sexually abused my little girl and then ran away with her. Later, she met Anna's father, her first husband. Since then she went from bad relationship to bad relationship.

This was when I first noticed that my little girl was nothing more than a confused angel, who thought she didn't deserve a good man. She's was a good woman Eric and this is all my fault. I gave her the anger and sadness." Eric with tears in his eyes. Put his hand on Hank's Shoulder.

"Hank, things happen that we can't change. This helps me to understand more of what Janeane was going through. No matter her past, your daughter is the love of my life and not a second goes by where I don't miss her. She never showed me signs or maybe I just missed them. She was always tired, but I thought it was natural after a woman gives birth. God, I feel so lost."

Hank looks at Eric.

" Look kid, you and those girls are the best thing that happened to her. In some odd way, she knew Anna and Layla were gonna be in the right hands. I'll never get the chance to make peace with my little girl. If it's alright with you, I would like to visit my granddaughters from time to time."

Eric nods yes. Hank gets up to leave, Eric gets up and hugs Hank. He breaks down and lets out a cry. He wipes his eyes and walks to the door.

"I'll show myself out. Take care."

Hearing the door, Anna walks out of the room.

"Is everything gonna be ok?"

Eric nods yes. Anna noticed her mother's photo in Eric's hand. "Are you ok?"

Eric exhales. "Yeah, I think."

Anna pauses.

"Can I go out with my friends?"

Eric takes a sip of coffee and clears his throat.

"Sure, where too?"

Anna looking around the kitchen.

"Just the mall, nothing special."

Eric pours himself more coffee. "Need any money?"

Anna shakes her head no. "Nah. I still have some left from babysitting."

Eric smiles.

"OK, enjoy and thanks for putting the baby to sleep."

Anna walks out the door. Layla begins to cry. Eric runs to the room and picks her up.

"Hey, hey shhhhhh it's ok. Daddy is here."

Eric holding the baby starts walking around the apartment. The baby will not stop crying. He tries feeding the baby and she refuses the bottle and continues to cry. Eric begins to pled.

"Shhhhh... Daddy's got you. Shhhhhh..."

Eric sits with the baby on the couch. As the baby cries, louder and louder, he begins to lose it.

"I know baby, I miss her too. "

The door opens and its Anna. Eric lost in the moment does not hear her.

"I forgot my..."

Anna sees Eric and Layla, crying. She stands and watches. She Sits next to Eric and puts her arm around his shoulder. Eric still sobbing.

"I can't make her stop crying."

Anna gently takes her sister in her hands and places her on her shoulder.

"It's gonna be ok. Shhhhh"

She pats Layla on the back and the baby lets out a burp. They both start to laugh. Anna hands Eric her sister back.

"Thank you, Anna. Go, your friends are waiting."

As Anna walks out the door she hears Eric talking to Layla.

"You have your mothers smile. It can light up a room."

* * *

Depression and Bipolar Support Alliance
Phone Number: 800-826-3632

Hopeline
Phone Number: 800-442-HOPE (4673)

Mental Health America – For a referral to specific mental health service or support program in your community
Phone Number: 800-969-NMHA (6642)

National Alliance on Mental Illness – Provides support, information, and referrals
Phone Number: 800-950-NAMI (6264)

National Association of Anorexia Nervosa and Associated Disorders
Phone Number: 847-831-3438

National Suicide Prevention Hotline
Phone Number: 800-273-TALK (8255)

Postpartum Support International
Phone Number: 800-994-4PPD (4773)

PPD Moms
Phone Number: 800-PPD-MOMS (800-773-6667)

S.A.F.E. Alternatives
Phone Number: 800-DONTCUT (800-366-8288)

EVEN THE STRONG, NEED A SHOULDER!